anythink

THE EVERLASTING PEAKS

LONE PEAK

STEWART FALLS

GOOB'S CAVE

UNCLE BUD'S PARK

JUMPER'S HOLE

POKEY'S PLACE

THE MEADOW

CHERRY CREEK

LILY'S BURROW

MS. HOOT'S GARDEN

TAGALONG ALLIE'S BURROW

Goob
and
His
Grandpa

To my precious daughter Rachel, who lived a beautiful life.
I'm so looking forward to our next trail ride.
—Sean Covey

In memory of Mark; you are missed.
—Stacy Curtis

SIMON & SCHUSTER BOOKS FOR YOUNG READERS
An imprint of Simon & Schuster Children's Publishing Division
1230 Avenue of the Americas, New York, New York 10020
Copyright © 2013 by Franklin Covey Co.
SIMON & SCHUSTER BOOKS FOR YOUNG READERS is a trademark of Simon & Schuster, Inc.
For information about special discounts for bulk purchases, please contact Simon & Schuster Special Sales at
1-866-506-1949 or business@simonandschuster.com.
The Simon & Schuster Speakers Bureau can bring authors to your live event. For more information or to book an
event, contact the Simon & Schuster Speakers Bureau at 1-866-248-3049 or visit our website at
www.simonspeakers.com.
Also available in a Simon & Schuster Books for Young Readers paper-over-board edition
Book design by Laurent Linn
The text for this book was set in Montara Gothic.
The illustrations for this book were rendered in pencil and watercolor.
Manufactured in China
0218 SCP
First Simon & Schuster Books for Young Readers paperback edition April 2018
2 4 6 8 10 9 7 5 3 1
The Library of Congress has cataloged the paper-over-board edition as follows:
Covey, Sean.
Goob and his grandpa / Sean Covey ; illustrated by Stacy Curtis. — First edition.
pages cm. — (The 7 habits of happy kids)
Summary: Goob's friends help him after his grandpa passes away.
ISBN 978-1-4424-7653-0 (hardcover : alk. paper) [1. Grandfathers—Fiction.
2. Death—Fiction. 3. Grief—Fiction. 4. Friendship—Fiction. 5. Bears—Fiction.
6. Animals—Fiction.] I. Curtis, Stacy, illustrator. II. Title.
PZ7.C8343Go 2014
[E]—dc23   2012046379
ISBN 978-1-5344-1584-3 (pbk)
ISBN 978-1-4424-7654-7 (eBook)

Goob
and
His
Grandpa

SEAN COVEY

Illustrated by Stacy Curtis

SIMON & SCHUSTER BOOKS FOR YOUNG READERS

New York   London   Toronto   Sydney   New Delhi

Goob Bear and his grandpa did everything together. They collected bugs at Fish-Eye Lake. They went on long hikes in the Far North Woods. They climbed trees and ate honey out of beehives. And they loved to wrestle on the living room floor.

"I love you, little Goober-head," Grandpa would say.

"I love you too, Grandpa," Goob would answer. "You're my best friend."

Later at recess, the gang got together.

"That stinks," said Lily. "I'll bet Goob misses him so much."

"I think we should go see him," said Pokey.

"I don't know if he'll want to see anyone right now," said Sophie.

"He's in mourning."

"Well," said Sammy, "what would you want if your grandpa died?"

"I'd want my fwens to be with me," said Tagalong Allie.

After school that day, everyone showed up at Goob's house.

He was sitting in his backyard, feeling sad.

"Hi, Goob," said Lily. "We came to see you."

"We're really sad about your grandpa," said Pokey. "He was

a really great guy."

"Thanks, Pokey. I'm sad too. I don't know if I'll ever be happy again," Goob said.

"If you're sad, then we're going to be sad with you," said Jumper.

They all huddled around Goob and they were all sad together for a long time. When it was time for the gang to go home, Goob felt a little better.

The next day everyone got together to make a plan. They knew that Goob needed friends, so each day after school, one of them would visit Goob.

On Tuesday, Sammy and Sophie showed up with their walking

sticks and took Goob on a long walk in the Far North Woods.

"That was invigorating," said Sophie.

"And fun, too," said Goob. "Grandpa loved to walk in the woods."

On Wednesday, Pokey took Goob to Fish-Eye Lake

to look for bugs.

On Thursday, Lily and Tagalong Allie helped Goob get some honey out of a beehive in a tree. Lily was scared of the bees, but Allie thought they were cute.

And on Friday, Jumper agreed to have a wrestling match with
Goob on his living room floor. It wasn't much fun for Jumper
because Goob kept squishing him. But Goob had a great time,
so Jumper was happy. Even Goob's mom didn't mind.

"I made you a cawd, too," said Tagalong Allie.

Allie opened up the card and read it out loud.

"Dear Goob, I'm so sad your gwanpa died. He was
your best fwend. Now me and Jumper and Pokey and
Wiwee and Sophie and Sammy will be your best fwends,
forevuh. I wuv you. Allie."

Jumper started crying and Goob gave him a hug.

"Thanks, Tagalong," said Goob. "That means everything to me. And thanks for being my friends, you guys. I'm going to miss my grandpa. But I don't feel so sad anymore."

PARENTS' CORNER

HABIT ⑦ —Sharpen the Saw: *Balance Feels Best*

I REMEMBER HOW SHAKEN I FELT WHEN MY FATHER PASSED AWAY. I KNEW I WOULD NEVER BE the same. After his death, I thought spending time alone was what I needed, but surprisingly, I found just the opposite to be true. Spending time with family and friends is what helped me most. The whole ordeal reminded me, once again, that in the great scheme of things relationships are all that really matter. Everything else is fleeting. No one on their deathbed ever wished they'd spent more time at the office.

But it's so easy to forget that in this frenetic world of ours. We get so busy driving that we don't take time to get gas. We get so caught up in our work and our carpools and our to-dos that we forget to spend quality, face-to-face time with the living, breathing human beings all around us. That is why Habit 7, Sharpen the Saw, was invented. It reminds us to take time to renew, to unwind, to take a walk, to laugh, to cry, to step back and think deeply, and to invest in our most important relationships.

In this story, be sure to highlight what a difference Goob's friends made at this difficult time in his life. Often the best thing we can do when a friend or family member is hurting is just to say we're sorry and to mourn with them. We don't need to say anything or fix something; we just need to be there for them so they know we care. May we ever be willing to sharpen our saws by regularly spending time with the people we love, in both good times and bad.

Up for Discussion

1. Why did Goob miss school?
2. Have you ever lost anyone close to you? How did it make you feel?
3. What do you like to do with your grandparents?
4. How did Goob's friends cheer him up?
5. If this happened to you, what would you like your friends to do to cheer you up?
6. When you feel sad, what do you like to do to feel better?

Baby Steps

1. Write a note to someone you know who has lost a loved one.
2. Talk to your parents about what you can do or will do when your family loses a loved one.
3. Go for a walk and look for beautiful things that make you happy.
4. Draw a picture of you and your grandparents and have your parents send it to them.
5. Learn more about your family's history by talking to your parents and grandparents about your ancestors.

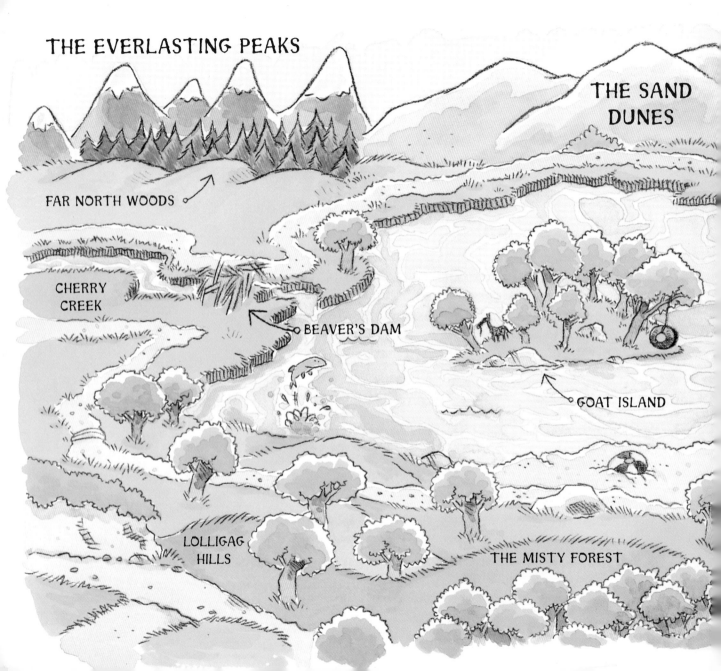

THE EVERLASTING PEAKS

THE SAND DUNES

FAR NORTH WOODS

CHERRY CREEK

BEAVER'S DAM

GOAT ISLAND

LOLLIGAG HILLS

THE MISTY FOREST